To Patty Hanna, museum buddy and friend extraordinaire —L.L.

To Mei Shuen —M.S.

AUTHOR'S NOTE

Wu Daozi (689–759) is known as perhaps China's greatest painter and was called the Sage of Painting during the T'ang dynasty (618–907), which was the height of classical Chinese civilization. He introduced the concept of depicting movement in figures and their clothing. His figures' scarves billowed, their robes swung, and their hair blew in the wind. Calligraphy was considered the highest art form at the time, but Wu Daozi almost single-handedly changed the way people viewed painting. He was highly praised in poems and essays by his contemporaries, but little has been written about him since.

Much of Wu Daozi's work consisted of murals on the walls of monasteries, palaces, and temples around Chang'an, the western capital of the T'ang dynasty, which is modern-day Xi'an. He produced around three hundred frescoes and more than a hundred scrolls; none of his frescoes survived.

This imagined version of Wu Daozi's life and work is pieced together from references I found in translations of T'ang poetry and essays and from the many known facts about life in Chang'an during T'ang times.

Text copyright © 2013 by Lenore Look • Jacket art and interior illustrations copyright © 2013 by Meilo So
All rights reserved. Published in the United States by Schwartz & Wade Books, an imprint of Random House Children's Books, a division of Random House, Inc., New York.
Schwartz & Wade Books and the colophon are trademarks of Random House, Inc.
Visit us on the Web! randomhouse.com/kids
Educators and librarians, for a variety of teaching tools, visit us at RHTeachersLibrarians.com

Library of Congress Cataloging-in-Publication Data
Look, Lenore. Brush of the gods / Lenore Look ;
[illustrated by] Meilo So Sandford. — 1st ed.
p. cm.
Summary: During the Tang dynasty, master painter Wu Daozi creates an extraordinary mural for the emperor.
ISBN 978-0-375-87001-9 (hc) — ISBN 978-0-375-97001-6 (glb)
1. Wu, Daozi, 689–759—Juvenile fiction. [1. Wu, Daozi, 689–759—Fiction. 2. Artists—Fiction. 3. Painting—Fiction. 4. China—History—Tang dynasty, 618–907—Fiction.] I. So, Meilo, ill. II. Title.
PZ7.L8682 Pai 2013 [E]—dc23 2012006442

The text of this book is set in Cg Adroit Light.
The illustrations were rendered in watercolor, ink, gouache, and colored pencil.
Book design by Rachael Cole

MANUFACTURED IN CHINA
10 9 8 7 6 5 4 3 2 1
First Edition

Brush of the Gods

BY Lenore Look ILLUSTRATIONS BY Meilo So

schwartz & wade books · new york

Wu Daozi looked at the brush in his hand and felt the soft hairs. They tickled.

"Soak your brush," said the stern old monk who was his teacher.

Daozi lowered it into a little saucer of water. He held his breath.

"Grind your ink," ordered the monk.

Daozi had not paid attention when their teacher showed them how. Now he watched the other children and copied as best he could.

They put a few drops of water on a flat stone and rubbed their ink pebbles one way, then the other. Black tears appeared between the stones.

"Sit up straight," urged the monk.

Daozi sat up.

"Hold your brush in line with your nose," said the monk.

Daozi stretched his neck so that his head floated like a moon above his brush. Then he looked straight down his nose.

"Press gently," said their teacher as he showed the class how to draw a smooth stroke from left to right, making a glistening number one in Chinese on an old tortoise shell.

"Calligraphy is the highest of the arts," he continued, slowly writing more numbers in beautiful strokes. "It reveals your character. Do it well and you will bring great honor to your family."

At the tip of Daozi's brush, a couple of worms crawled out.

The boy gasped.

"What's that?" asked the monk.

"Worms," said Daozi.

"Worms?"

Silence.

"Your worms are beautiful, but you must learn your *characters*."

So Daozi tried again.

This time, blades of grass came from his brush.

The other children giggled.

"You must try harder," said the monk.

Concentration folded Daozi's body into a tight little fan.

Then, with a flick of his wrist, a straight line dropped out like the back of a robe . . . then curved and squiggled and fell into a hem.

"I love calligraphy!" he cried.

"That's not calligraphy," the monk sighed.

Each day something new and surprising dripped out of Daozi's brush. His straight lines splintered into trees. His hooks caught fish.

His dots burst into eyes, then pigs and monkeys. From a stroke, a horse's tail flew by.

The boy drew on walls everywhere—at temples, teahouses, and the silk bazaar. He even drew on the big wall surrounding the city.

Dancing peonies.

Flying Buddhas sewn into the sky.

Clouds stitched around them.

All who saw were amazed.

"Exquisite," said a lady in a sedan chair.

"It's a gift," said a nun, bowing low.

"He has flying sleeves!" said a boy with a kite.

Indeed, Daozi painted so fast that his sleeves looked like wings spread in flight.

Admirers began to leave coins for the painter they now called Flying Sleeves. Bowls of rice. Fruit. Even a chicken.

Daozi ran to the monastery with their gifts to feed the poor. The monks were very pleased.

Every day Daozi painted to his heart's content. With
one eye wide open, the other in a dream, he painted
so much that he knew not whether the sun was up or
down or whether he was standing or sitting.

Seasons passed.

The more Daozi painted, the better he got, until one day he painted a butterfly so exquisite and delicate that he couldn't take his eyes off it.

The longer he admired it, the more real it looked.

Then a wing moved, just a little, when the wind blew.

"What?" said Daozi. He leaned closer.

And suddenly, the butterfly rose and floated away like burnt paper above a fire.

"*Aiiiiyaaaah!*" the painter exclaimed. "I must have only *imagined* I painted it, when in fact a *real* butterfly had landed there."

Quickly Daozi painted another. This time, it was a butterfly he knew by name—the majestic Leopard Lacewing.

Its wings glistened in the afternoon light.

The boy blinked.
The butterfly winked.

Before Daozi could cup his hand around his beautiful creation, it soared away.

"Come back!" he shouted. "You belong in my painting!"

But butterflies don't listen.

Quickly Daozi painted a camel and ran to tell the monks.

When they returned, it too was gone.

"My painted camels are so real they can walk away!"
cried Daozi.

The monks shook their heads. "It is better to paint
than to boast," said one.

That day no one left rice or money for Daozi. The great city wall was bare, though people could hear his brush slapping and sweeping against the bricks.

Daozi's birds fluttered away. His horses galloped into the
mountains. Even his carriages rolled down the street and
straight out of town. All that he painted disappeared.

Daozi wept.

His admirers also vanished.

All except the children.

"His pigeon landed on my
head!" one beggar child cried.

"I can chirp along with his crickets," marveled
another. *"Chirp chirp!"*

The children followed Daozi everywhere. Tattered
and shoeless, they formed a hedge around their
friend. As long as he painted, they forgot their hunger.

Years passed.
The crowds grew.
The children
brought their own
children to marvel
at Daozi's works.

Inside the central gate of the Temple of Renewed Virtue, people came rushing in when he painted the halo on a Buddha. They gasped when his brush swept with the force and brilliance of a comet.

In the Inner Hall, Daozi painted five dragons whose scaly armor moved in flight.

In temples throughout the city, waterfalls spilled from his imagined mountainsides.

"*Aaaaaah,*" someone cried. "This man is no ordinary painter. He holds the brush of the gods!"

One day, the emperor himself came.

Upon seeing the five dragons, he drew his sword.

At the peonies, he bent and sniffed.

From the gushing water, he drank.

"Master Wu," the emperor finally said. "I shall
give you an entire wall of the palace on which
to paint a grand masterpiece. No one may
see it until you are done."

It was the greatest honor Daozi could
imagine. He bowed deeply.

But a
masterpiece
takes many years to create.
By the time the mural was
finished, the great artist
had grown old.

At last, the royal unveiling ceremony began.
An orchestra of seven hundred instruments played.

When the drapery was pulled away, mountains pierced holes into the sky. Bamboo swayed. Birds flew. Horses galloped in the distance. There were nine thousand, nine hundred and ninety-nine things to behold. The painting was as brilliant as fresh-fallen snow.

The crowd fell silent.

The emperor bowed.

The moon wept.

Drenched in the moon's silver tears, the master painter
added a shimmering archway and cried out in a loud voice,

"It is Paradise!
Follow me!"

And before anyone could move, the man with the brush of the
gods walked straight into his painting . . . and disappeared.

*L*egend has it that Wu Daozi never died— he merely walked into his final painting, a landscape commissioned by Emperor Xuanzong, and disappeared. The work, painted on a palace wall, did not survive. The year of Wu's disappearance varies—sometimes it is given as 759, sometimes 762 or 792—the uncertainty being further proof, they say, that he cheated death.